Orion

Shifter Ink, Volume 3

S L Davies

Published by S L Davies, 2022.

ORION

First edition. September 15, 2022.

Copyright © 2022 S L Davies.

ISBN: 979-8215802106

Written by S L Davies.

Prologue

O rion

"What do you reckon about three Shifter Ink people being mated now," Sahara said as we drove towards Chase's home that he now shared with Bronson.

I sighed. "I'm jealous as fuck," I said with a chuckle. It was true. I was jealous. I'd longed to find my mate since I knew what mates were. I didn't have a family; having grown up in the foster system, I didn't know my parents or if I had siblings. And I got moved around so often that I could never make lifelong friends.

On the plus side, I had my Shifter Ink family. Chase, Brenton, and I had always been close, considering we all had something in common. We were vampires. But now that they were all finding their mates, I would see them less and less.

"I'm jealous too," Sahara said with a sigh.

"Things not working out with Rupert?" I asked. Fucking stupid name. I hated the guy. Sleazy was an understatement. Sahara deserved so much better, but she came from a wealthy human family that was all about status. The fact that Sahara was a tattooist was shameful enough for her family. But they were satisfied as long as she put her head down and showed up to the right events with Rupert by her side.

Sahara sighed again. "I can't fucking stand him. Now my parents are talking about us getting married."

"What?" I barked out as I turned in the passenger seat to stare at her. "You're not." Sahara shrugged her shoulders, and the sadness on her face said everything. "Oh, Sar, please. You know that you don't have to do it. You make good money at Shifter Ink; you could walk away and be alright."

Sahara nodded as her eyes welled with tears. "I know. It's just that even though sometimes I hate my parents so much, I still love them. I still believe that maybe one day they will be proud of me if I would just do as they expect."

"Sahara, you can't go so far as marrying a man you hate. It's only going to end in disaster."

Sahara shrugged her shoulders. "I know. I just don't know what else to do. It's tricky, you know."

I shook my head. "No. I don't know. But I can sort of understand."

Sahara gave me a weak smile. I didn't understand. I would tell my parents where to stick their wedding ideas if it were me. But it wasn't me. I wasn't human and didn't even have parents, so I couldn't understand the pressure on Sahara's shoulders.

As we rounded the corner, I saw Chase's house with various cars parked out the front and on the street. I knew that Bronson was inviting his friends to meet us too. Bronson, like me, had grown up in the foster system. Unfortunately, those of us who weren't wanted by our biological parents often found ourselves not adopted. People didn't wish for supernatural children. We were too much work.

"Wow, looks like it's going to be a good turnout," Sahara said as she pulled into the car spot on the side of the road.

"Sure does. I'm kinda curious to meet Bronson's friends."

Sahara grinned and nodded her head. "Me too. He has told me a lot about them. He seems so proud of them. I like that."

"Me too," I replied as I swung open the passenger door and stepped out of the car. I didn't bother to own my own car, I lived only a few doors down from Shifter Ink, and if I needed to go anywhere further out, there was either public transport or I was traveling with Shifter Ink members, so we pooled together.

Sahara and I walked up to the front door, where a few other Shifter Ink members had just arrived.

"Hey," Merrigan said with a grin before she pulled me into a tight hug.

I greeted all my friends before walking in through the open door and into the living room, where I came to a complete standstill. My eyes widened, and my mouth dropped open. I scanned my eyes around the room, trying to find where the smell of blueberries and marshmallows was coming from. There was no mistaking that scent.

My eyes landed on a tall man with a shock of red hair, watching me with equal amounts of wonder and desire on his face. The room suddenly fell quiet, and I heard Bronson asking what was happening.

"You're my mate," I said quietly.

The man nodded his head. "I'm Roddy."

"I'm Orion," I replied. "Roddy, do you want to be my mate?"

Roddy bit into his bottom lip and nodded his head. "Yes," he said barely above a whisper.

Without another thought, I stepped forward and took Roddy by the hand. The minute our hands touched, it felt like electricity shooting up and down my body. Tingles ran all over my skin. I found my mate. My fucking mate. Best day ever.

Chapter One

Roddy

What the hell was going on? Was this even real? My brain was spinning as I drove towards my home, with Orion sitting in the passenger seat of my car. I was supposed to spend time with one of my best friends, Bronson, as we met his mate. I never expected that my mate would literally walk in the door.

I'd said yes to Orion immediately, but now that we were heading back to my house, fear filled me. Mating with Orion meant that he would have to see my body. He would see the scars that dotted my skin. My legs were scarred from the many operations I had over the years, but the rest of the wounds. They were caused by me.

I was embarrassed about it, but at the same time, I did it to cope. I cut myself when my stress got too much. My cutting started when I was fourteen years old. I was going through puberty and trying to understand what it was to be an omega that no one wanted. I didn't have a pack or anyone around me who truly understood what it was like to be a shifter.

At school, I was bullied for my red hair. I was called a Ranga and teased mercilessly. Add to that; I couldn't run or walk like normal kids. I had a limp, and my back legs were slightly twisted even when I was shifted. The pain in my legs and hips worsened as I grew, especially over winter. It meant that I couldn't do a lot of what others did.

As a young man, I'd decided I would never get involved in a relationship because I didn't want them to see my scars. I'd once been vulnerable in front of a guy at school. He asked why I never wore shorts, even when it was hot. I'd explained to him about the scars. He asked to see them. I'd lifted the legs of my pants up so he could see them, only for him to laugh his ass off like it was the funniest thing he'd ever seen.

After that, he and his friends called me all sorts of names. It hurt. I had people asking me if I was slow or mental. I didn't care if someone had issues with their mind, but it still hurt that people would use my physical disability against me. If our P.E. teacher suggested that we do some running sports, there was always at least one jerk to announce how I should sit out because I couldn't run.

I was always picked last for all the sports teams. In the end, I just stopped showing up for sports classes altogether. Our careers teacher had been fantastic, and she'd asked me straight out if it was because of my legs that I'd been skipping class. I'd opened up to her and told her everything. After that, she said I could go to her office and work on homework and still pass P.E.

That made things a lot easier; it was one class I didn't have to see the assholes who made my life a living hell. But now here I was driving through the streets of Lalbert towards Winchester, where my house was hidden amongst the forest on a large property. I liked being so far out of town. I hated the idea of people just rocking up at my house.

The only people that ever visited me were Bronson, Zale, Sarria, and my manager, Brian. If I had meetings with new clients, I always travelled to them. I liked having my sanctuary. I valued my privacy primarily because of fear, but I just wanted quiet. If there was too much noise around me, I got anxious.

"You are very quiet. Are you having second thoughts?" Orion asked, breaking into my thoughts.

I quickly glanced at the vampire and bit my lip before shaking my head. "No. Look, I don't know how else to tell you this, but I have a lot of scars on my body," I blurted.

We probably should have discussed it before leaving Bronson and Chase's home. Still, I'd rather Orion know before he saw me without my clothes on.

"Why would that matter?" Orion asked.

"They are ugly."

Orion fell silent, and when I glanced over at him again, he was frowning down into his lap. He remained silent and stared down at his lap until I pulled off the road and down my driveway's long dirt road.

Once I pulled up in front of my garage, I killed the engine and looked over at Orion. If he didn't want to mate with me, I'd understand. Slowly he lifted his head and reached out his hand, snagging mine. He took my hand and placed my fingers under his shirt over his chest. Gently he guided my fingers up and down over his chest, and I could feel a large raised scar.

I frowned. "What is that from?" I asked. The scar was down the center of his chest and about ten centimeters long.

"When I was twelve, I had to have open heart surgery. I'd been a sick kid for years; my foster parents thought it was because I was a vampire and needed blood. But that wasn't the problem. As it turned out, I had a hole in one of the valves. It was discovered when I was twelve and had a heart attack at school."

My eyes widened, and I gasped. "A heart attack? Shit."

Orion smiled and nodded his head. "Yeah. I don't really remember it. But apparently, it scared the shit out of the kids in my class. One minute I was sitting at my desk, and the next, I was clutching my chest and unconscious on the ground. I woke up in hospital with wires sticking out of me and some dead boy's heart in my chest."

"It helped; you are healthy now," I pointed out.

Orion sighed and shook his head. "The first heart didn't. Two weeks later, I had to get another heart. This time it worked. But I had to be in hospital for months, and by the time I returned to school, I had this huge scar down my chest."

"At least you could hide it," I said miserably.

Orion nodded his head. "Yeah. But you obviously are doing alright, hiding yours."

I shrugged one shoulder. "Yeah, I guess so. My scars are on my legs and arms. My legs are from surgeries. I was born with club feet. My arms, though. I did them myself."

Orion didn't say anything but nodded his head. I expected to see him recoil in disgust, but he didn't. He continued to keep my eye contact.

"How aren't you going into heat?" he asked suddenly.

I snorted at the sudden change in subject. "I'm on heat suppressants."

"That makes sense. Look, Roddy, I understand that the scars might seem ugly to you, but they don't change anything for me. I want you to be my mate. If you don't want to be mine, that's okay; I will walk away. Well, I will ask you to drive me back to Bronson's, but I won't ever force myself on you."

I breathed in deeply through my nose before slowly letting it out. *Was I really going to do this?*

"I want to mate with you," I finally responded. It was fate. I couldn't turn my back on it.

Chapter Two

O rion

I got the distinct impression that Roddy was struggling with himself. He'd been silent the entire trip back to his house. It made a bit more sense when he'd opened up to me about his scars. He was someone who had a lot of body image issues. I couldn't say I understood it, but I was going to try. I thought he was gorgeous. Scars weren't something that I ever cared about.

In my mind, scars were stories on your skin, not that much different from tattoos. But the scars were proof of the battles we've been through. I was no longer ashamed of the scar on my chest. It was actually Burgess who taught it to me. I'd gone to him and asked him to tattoo over the scar. He told me he could but then asked if I really wanted to cover it because my scar told me just how strong I was.

After talking to Burgess about everything, I changed my mind. Instead, I chose to keep my chest free of ink. I wanted to wear my scar proudly. I was strong. I'd survived not only a heart attack but being bullied and rejected by people whom I'd thought were my friends. I stayed, and I thrived.

I never wished anything bad on those people that hurt me during my school days, but I wanted to show how much I could overcome to be better than they ever thought I would.

I followed Roddy into his house on the very outskirts of Lalbert. The house was massive and surrounded by forest. If I was driving past, I'd have never known there was even a house back here. The place was a beautiful big log cabin. Stepping inside was equally as gorgeous as the outside.

"So, um, welcome," Roddy said. His cheeks blushed. I couldn't work out if it was that he was ashamed of his home or just wasn't comfortable having people in it.

Slowly I stepped forward and encroached on Roddy's space. His lips popped open as he watched me. I could smell his arousal and knew

I wasn't the only one affected. I'd been curious that he wasn't going into heat around me, but it made sense when he'd told me he was on suppressants. But I knew that he was still as horny as I was.

I thought my cock was about to burst through my jeans. I gently cupped Roddy's cheeks and looked down into his eyes. His pupils were blown, and he licked over his bottom lip as he watched me. Slowly, giving him enough time to pull away, I lowered my mouth to hover over his.

"I'm going to kiss you now," I warned quietly.

Roddy nodded his head. I moved the rest of the way before covering his lips with mine. At first, they were sweet small kisses. But then I felt Roddy's tongue slip out to lick over the crease of my lips. I met his tongue with mine and groaned as his taste hit my senses.

Stroking my hands down over his back to his hips, I pulled him closer to me, grinding our cocks together. He was hard, and from the bulge, I could tell he was as well endowed as me. I was versatile and loved a cock in my ass as much as I loved my cock in a man's ass. Fuck, I wanted him inside me at some stage.

I broke the kiss only when I couldn't breathe any longer. When I looked into Roddy's eyes, they were filled with lust.

"Do you want to mate with me, Little Wolf?" I asked. Little Wolf was probably a stupid nickname for Roddy. He was as tall as I was, which was a little over six feet. But he was slender and almost fragile, so it fit.

"Yes," Roddy whispered.

I growled as I leaned forward and started to kiss his neck. Roddy gasped and groaned as he moved his head to give me more access to his neck. The scent of Roddy's blood flowing through his veins was so sweet, like candy floss. Being a born vampire, I didn't need blood to live, but it was one of those things that were a bit of a delicacy. The fact that Roddy was my mate made his blood more like crack.

"Take me to your bedroom, Little Wolf," I said, lifting my face from his neck. I wanted him. I wanted to feel him, taste him, bathe in him.

Roddy nodded and took my hand in his as he led me out of the living room, down a short hall to a bedroom with the most enormous bed I'd ever seen. The large window looked out over the forest that surrounded the house. I could imagine how beautiful this was to wake up to in the morning. Or lay in on a stormy evening.

"I'm going to strip you from your clothes now," I warned. Knowing how Roddy felt about his scars, I wanted to give him plenty of warning before I saw them. I tried to prepare him and give him a chance to say no.

Roddy sucked in a deep breath and bit into his bottom lip. He finally nodded his head. I reached down to the hem of his shirt and tugged. Lifting it over his head, I looked down at my mate. His chest was chiseled and covered in a smattering of red hair. His shoulders were covered in freckles. When I looked back at his face, it was flushed red, and he wouldn't look me in the eyes.

I ran my fingers along the scars etched into his arms. Some that were far deeper than others. Leaning forward, I pressed my lips against each spot and kissed them. I wanted to show Roddy that I wasn't horrified or disgusted by the scars. With nimble fingers, I undid his jeans and pushed them down over his hips to his thighs. Roddy used the toe of his shoe to kick one off and then the other.

I kneeled as I slipped his jeans off. The scars on his legs were hidden behind thick blonde hairs. They were surgical scars and told the story of his life with this disability. I slipped one sock from his foot before taking the other. His feet were still somewhat turned, but I could see where doctors had attempted to straighten his legs.

Slowly I skimmed my hands over his feet and legs, carefully running featherlight touches over each scar. I watched Roddy's face, who stared down at me with embarrassment and lust in his eyes. His cock was hard and weeping, and I could tell he was battling with himself about whether he should enjoy it or hideaway.

I wanted him to realize just how beautiful he was and that the scars most definitely didn't make him ugly. I knew that I wouldn't be able to do that with words. This was going to take time and healing, and that was something I could give both of us.

Chapter Three

R oddy
My emotions were all over the place. On the one hand, I was mortified as Orion skimmed his fingers over my scars, but at the same time, I was in so much awe. He didn't recoil. He didn't react in any way that I'd expected. Instead, he gently caressed each scar with reverence. I felt somewhat attractive and less like a monster for the first time.

I watched Orion as he stroked his hands up my thighs. He leaned forward and brushed his nose against my hip, placing small kisses along my skin. My cock was so hard it almost hurt. Slick was leaking a steady drip, and my thighs were soaked.

Orion moved closer to my cock, and I bit into my bottom lip. I'd never been with anyone before. I'd always been too ashamed of my body, so I had hidden it. I'd turned that part of me off that wanted intimacy. But the way Orion worked over my body made me want it more than ever.

I felt Orion's tongue stroke the underside of my cock, my toes curled, and my hands moved automatically as they tangled through Orion's blonde hair. He blew warm air over my balls, which jumped at the attention. Slowly he started to lick over the sensitive skin. My eyes rolled, and I let out a long moan. It was almost too much, but not enough all in one.

"Fuck, you taste good," Orion moaned.

I looked down to see him watching me as he opened his lips and took the head of my cock into his mouth.

"Oh god," I groaned. I'd never felt anything like it. And I knew damn well there would be no way I would last. Orion moaned around my cock as he lathered it with his tongue, bobbing up and down.

He took my balls in his hands, gently rolling them. I hissed at the overwhelming sensation. Tingles spread across my body, and my balls got tight. The pleasure started in the base of my spine and moved outwards across my entire body.

"I'm gonna cum," I warned.

Orion sucked my cock deeper down his throat. Tears prickled at my eyes as pleasure tore from my body, wave after wave, washed over me. I roared as I felt my cock spasm, filling Orion's mouth with my seed.

I was breathing heavily as I looked down at Orion. He licked up and down my shaft before planting a kiss on the head. Still stiff and weeping, I bit into my bottom lip.

"I've never experienced anything like that," I whispered.

Orion smiled. "I hope that means it was good."

I chuckled and nodded my head. "You've no idea just how good."

Orion's smile took over his face as he stood and pressed his lips against mine. I could taste myself on his tongue as he kissed me. I thought I should be disgusted, but it turned me on further.

"I want to mate with you," I said, looking up into Orion's eyes.

Orion nodded his head and smiled wickedly. He quickly stripped out his clothes, dumping them on the floor beside mine. The scar on his chest was prominent and the only place he wasn't tattooed. I wondered briefly if he'd done that on purpose.

Orion took my hand and led me over to the bed. "I need to ask you something," he said. I looked up at him as I sat down on the bed. "Do you only bottom?"

I frowned and shrugged my shoulders. "To be honest, I don't know. The only thing I've ever had in my ass was my dildo when I went through my heat. I've never been with anyone else."

Orion's eyes flared as if he liked my answer. "I like to bottom as well sometimes."

"Yeah?" I didn't know what it was about the thought of fucking Orion's ass, but it turned me on beyond anything I could ever imagine.

"Yeah."

"Do you want me to top you now?" I asked.

Orion bit into his bottom lip and nodded his head. "Yeah, I think I do."

My breathing hitched at the idea. I stood from the bed and rummaged through my drawers to find my bottle of lube. I may not have been with anyone, but lube always made jerking off feel better.

Orion smiled as I handed him the bottle. "I want you to prepare me," he said, holding the bottle.

"I don't know how," I admitted. My cheeks blazed with embarrassment at admitting to this beautiful man that I had no idea what I was doing.

Orion took my hand and squirted a large wad of lube onto my fingers. He laid back on the bed, lifting his legs, so he was open to me. "Pour some lube over my ass, then slowly work in a finger, then another; once you've got me loose enough to take three fingers, then fuck me."

I bit into my bottom lip and nodded my head. I could do this.

Chapter Four

O rion

I didn't know why I suddenly so desperately wanted Roddy inside me. But I needed it. I needed to feel his cock buried in me while we mated. He slowly skimmed his fingers down over my ass, and my eyes rolled at the feeling of him there. It was exactly what I needed.

Slowly and with an uncertain look, he pushed one finger past the tight ring of muscles. I hissed at that first intrusion.

"Did I hurt you?" he asked suddenly.

I shook my head and smiled. "No. Curl your fingers, find my prostate," I instructed.

Roddy did as I instructed; the minute his finger rolled over my prostate, I let out a long moan.

"Is that it?" he asked.

"Oh, fuck yes, that's it."

My cock leaked a steady stream of precum as he worked his finger in and out of me. My toes were curling, and I desperately wanted him inside me, but I also wanted Roddy to be ready. When he'd stretched me with three fingers, my body was ready to start climbing the walls with need.

"Please, Roddy, I need your cock," I pleaded.

Roddy, who had been watching his fingers moving in and out of me with interest, nodded and took the bottle of lube. The minute he removed his fingers from my ass, I regretted asking him to stop. I needed him.

I didn't have to wait long before I felt the head of his cock pushing past the ring of muscles deep inside me.

"Fuck yes," I groaned as he bottomed out.

"Oh god, that feels so good," Roddy groaned.

"Fuck me, Little Wolf, fuck me hard," I pleaded.

Roddy didn't need to be told twice as he snapped his hips. Every time his cock hit my prostate, it pulled me higher and higher. I clawed at my thighs that trembled under the weight of my pleasure. My alpha was roaring, desperate to make Roddy ours.

My fangs grew longer, and the scent of Roddy's blood overwhelmed me. I looked up at my mate. His eyes that had been grey were changed. His wolf was close to the front. His eyes were now almost hazel and looked like they held a wildfire inside them.

"Make me yours," I cried.

Roddy roared and bent forward. The minute his incisors bit into my chest; pleasure washed me away. I cried out as cum spewed from my cock. My eyes widened as I felt Roddy lock inside me with a knot. Roddy was an omega. He shouldn't have a knot. No sooner had I had that thought than my alpha took over. I leaned forward on autopilot, biting into Roddy. His blood was sweeter than any candy I'd ever eaten.

I pulled back and bit into my wrist, and blood started to bloom. I placed it over Roddy's lips, who suckled in the answer I needed to complete the mateship. Roddy's roar of pleasure echoed throughout the room. His body was locked tight in mine as I felt the warmth of his cum fill me.

We slowly started to fall back to reality, and I realized that he was indeed locked hard inside me.

"Um, Roddy," I drew my mate's attention.

"Yeah?" he asked, looking down at me lazily. His face was so peaceful, and I didn't want to worry him, but this just wasn't normal.

"Why do you have a knot?"

Roddy's eyes widened, and he gasped. "Holy shit. I have a knot. Why do I have a knot? I'm an omega. I shouldn't have a knot."

"I know. I don't mind, but it's kind of strange."

Roddy nodded his head. I could see panic taking over and felt horrible for bringing it up.

I stroked my hands up and down his back. "Hey, Little Wolf, don't worry. It will be fine. This is something we can look into, okay."

Roddy bit into his bottom lip and frowned. "Yeah. Would you still want me, though, if I wasn't an omega?"

"Are you fucking kidding me? I'd want you even if you were an alien with two dicks and three heads."

Roddy barked out a laugh and shook his head. "You're a joker."

I smirked. "I love to make those I love to laugh."

Roddy sighed. "I'm not usually one that laughs too easily."

"That's okay, you know. We all are individuals, and that is what makes this world so awesome. We aren't all the same."

Roddy nodded. "Maybe. So, what do we do now?"

"Well, considering there is no chance of going anywhere right now, why don't we get to know each other?"

"Sure," he said with a smile. "What's your favorite color, favorite food, and favorite singer."

I hummed and tapped my chin. "My favorite color is red. My favorite food is most definitely pizza, and as for the singer, I love The Doors. What about you?"

"My favorite color is purple, my favorite food is roast pork, and I love The Doors too, but my favorite would be Johnny Cash."

"The biggest question, though, is, does pineapple go on pizza?"

Roddy snorted. "Fuck yeah."

"Yes, I've found me a winner," I crowed. Roddy leaned forward and kissed me. Our tongues tangled, and I felt myself growing hard. Roddy moved slightly, and I felt his knot unlock from me.

"How about you fuck me now?" he purred.

"With pleasure," I said as I rolled on the bed and flipped him to his back.

Chapter Five

R oddy

Even though we didn't leave the bedroom for at least three days, all bar eating and going to the bathroom, the worry that I'd been able to develop a knot was still firmly in my mind. *What the hell?* I'd gone into heat for the first time when I was seventeen. I knew I was an omega; I was pretty sure I was. And I produce slick. Alpha's didn't create slick. But I'd never had my reproductive organs seen to, so I couldn't say for sure.

"Are you alright?" Orion asked as he stretched in the bed. We'd just finished another round of fucking. When Orion said that he liked bottoming, he wasn't lying. The man was insatiable. That wasn't a complaint either. I realized how much I'd missed out on all these years.

"Yeah, I was thinking about the fact that I can knot. I shouldn't be able to do that," I said.

Orion stroked his hand over my back before pulling me into his side. "Want to make an appointment to see the doctor? Get some tests done to find out a possible reason?"

I nodded. "I think that would be a good idea. I'm just worried; what if it means we can't have kids."

Orion went silent for a moment. "I'm not going to lie and say it would be fine because it would be sad that we couldn't have our own children. But you and I both know what it is like to grow up in the foster system. Would adopting a child be that bad?"

I hummed and turned to face my mate. "You're right. Would you be opposed to a child with special needs?"

Orion smiled and shook his head. "Absolutely not. I am happy if you are happy. But first, let's focus on whether or not we even need to go down the route straight away. I mean, even if you can have children, we can also look into adopting."

I breathed in deeply and nodded my head. "I'd like that."

I didn't realize how much I wanted children until just now. And Orion was right; even if I couldn't have children from my own body, there was adoption. Something about adopting a child who was rejected because they had special needs was more appealing to me. Maybe it was because I was once that child. But I wanted to show a kid love and that not everyone rejected them because they were different.

Orion pressed his lips against mine, and I moaned into the kiss. I wasn't sure that my cock even had it in him to get hard. Orion seemed to think the same as he broke the kiss.

"Want to shower, get dressed and go out for breakfast? I imagine that Bronson is pretty eager to hear from you, and no doubt my workmates are too," he said with a chuckle.

"Oh shit. Bronson. I feel horrible; we literally walked out on his party."

Orion chuckled again. "I think he probably understood. If he had met Chase at the start of the convention, I feel that the two of them would have left straight away."

I stretched and flipped the blanket from my body before standing on shaky legs. It had been a while since I'd been this active, and every muscle in my body was aching. By the way, Orion winced as he sat up; I knew he was feeling the same way.

"I think I'm going to have to take a few days off bottoming again," Orion snorted.

I laughed and nodded my head. "I think my poor little man needs a break; I'm surprised he doesn't have blisters."

"I'd kiss it better."

My cock tried its hardest to give a slight twitch in excitement before he gave up and remained flaccid. He'd fought the good fight; he deserved the rest.

I walked into the bathroom and flipped on the shower taps, watching as the room slowly filled with steam. Orion joined me, and together we showered. There was nothing sexual about the shower, but it was still such an intimate moment. I never thought about how beautiful mateship could be. But Mother fate had outdone herself. She had chosen me the perfect mate, and I couldn't be happier.

Once we were showered and dressed, I drove first to Orion's house so he could change his clothes, seeing as he didn't have a spare set of clothes. We had to talk about what we would do logistically about our living situation. Orion told me he owned the small apartment in the center of Lalbert, but I knew I'd struggle to live in the city. It was too noisy and crowded. Not to mention that I had all my equipment and everything I needed to work at home. Orion didn't seem to be fazed about any of it. He was such an easygoing guy, and I wondered if that was really how he was or whether it was an easy mask to wear.

After leaving Orion's house, we went down the road to Shifter Ink, where we were greeted with wolf whistles and cheers, making me laugh.

Bronson stood and pulled me into his arms. "Congratulations, Roddy. If there is anyone more deserving of love from Orion, it's you."

"Thank you," I said quietly.

Bronson looked at me with a frown and cocked his head. He'd always been able to see when I was struggling. He had this innate ability. I didn't know if he was psychic or more in tune with me because we were best friends, but he could always tell when something was going on in my mind before anyone else did.

"What's wrong?" he whispered.

Orion was busy talking to the other members of Shifter Ink, which gave me a chance to whisper to Bronson. I got the impression that Orion had done it on purpose, knowing that my best friend would want all the details.

"I knotted Orion," I blurted.

Bronson frowned with confusion before his eyes widened. "But you're an omega."

"I know. I don't know why it happened. But it did, every time."

Bronson leaned forward and sniffed. "You still smell like an omega, but something else is happening. Something that wasn't there before the mating."

"What do you mean?"

Bronson shook his head. "I don't know exactly. But your scent. It's different. I just assumed it was because you had mated. But now that you told me you got a knot, it makes me wonder if it isn't something else."

I sighed and shrugged my shoulders. "I'm going to make an appointment to see a doctor. It might mean that I can't have children."

Bronson winced. He'd sent me a text telling me he was pregnant and excited about having a baby.

"It's not all bad. I talked to Orion about it, and he suggested we adopt a special-needs child."

Bronson's face morphed into a smile. "I love that idea. You would make a fantastic father."

I hugged my friend and sighed. A father was something I had no idea how to be, but I was prepared to learn.

Chapter Six

O^{rion}

"So, what's it like being a mated man?" Burgess asked with a grin.

"It is the best thing ever." the smile on my face was genuine. I felt like the luckiest man in the world.

"So, you'll be the next to become a dad," Brenton teased.

I shrugged my shoulders. "If it happens, it happens."

Brenton narrowed his eyes as he looked at me with scrutiny. I knew that he would pick up on my hesitation. Until we had an appointment with the doctor to find out why Roddy was able to get a knot, I wouldn't get excited at the prospect of having my own children. Not that an adopted child would be any less mine, they just wouldn't share my DNA.

"Burgess, do you mind if I take the rest of the week off? We have a few things that have to be sorted out," I said, changing the subject.

Burgess waved his hand. "Of course, that's fine. What are you going to be doing about living arrangements?"

I owned a house in Lalbert a few doors down from Shifter Ink. I'd picked it up as a bargain, with a shop and an apartment. I'd rented the shop out to a young girl, Talisha, who wanted to use it for a dress shop while I lived in the apartment.

"I'll probably rent my place and then move in with Roddy. He has all his equipment for his work out there."

"You're going to need to buy a car," Chase teased.

I chuckled and nodded my head. "Or maybe a motorbike."

"And if you have kids? How are you going to get them about on a motorbike." Chase snorted.

"It works for the Devil's Advocates guys," I argued.

"They all have cars, too," Burgess pointed out.

I shrugged my shoulders and chuckled. "I will look at a car in a little bit. I'll work it out. Anyway, I better dash; we've got some appointments to get to and sort out some things."

"No worries, man," Burgess said before pulling me into a hug. "If you need anything, let me know."

Chase hugged me, followed by Sloane, Sahara, Briony, and Merrigan. Brenton smiled and wrapped his arm around my shoulder as he walked towards the front door.

"Right, spill, what's going on?" he asked.

I chuckled. "You are too damned smart for your own good," I said before inhaling deeply. "Look, I don't know that it is necessarily anything. But we are going to make appointments to see a doctor with Roddy. He was able to knot."

Brenton's eyes widened. "Yeah, okay, that is different. Not something I've heard of happening before in an omega."

"Me neither. He won't say anything, but he is nervous."

Brenton nodded his head. "I can imagine that he is pretty nervous about whether he can have children or not."

"Yeah. That and the body image issues he has going on; I'm just worried that this will be a step too far for him. He struggles a lot more than I think even Bronson knows."

Brenton winced and nodded his head. "There are a lot of doctors out there that can help, not just physically but mentally too. Make sure that you use them."

I nodded my head. "Yeah, I will," I said as I glanced over at Roddy who was standing talking to Bronson still. "I think I'm falling in love with him."

Brenton chuckled. "I wouldn't be surprised that you are falling in love with him. It tends to happen when Mother fate steps in."

I smirked. "So, how are things with Hendrix?"

Brenton sighed. "Our relationship is good, but he still struggles. Every day is a fight to not go back to drugs. Some days are harder for him than others."

"He hasn't tripped up?"

Brenton shook his head. "No. But he's come close a couple of times. Thankfully he has had enough mind to ring me and talk through the problems or to call his sponsor. But I'm just worried that one day mine or his sponsor's voices aren't enough."

"Yeah, I can get that. Is he still seeing Alexandria?" I asked. Alexandria was a psychologist who worked with the Devil's Advocates and the omegas they rescued. She was a fantastic person, from what I knew about her.

Brenton nodded his head. "Yeah. He has a lot of trouble opening up about the things that happened to him during his childhood, and that's when he most wants to use when he thinks of the events of his childhood."

I sighed. "I can't imagine it is easy."

Brenton shook his head. "No. I wish I could reach into him and heal it all. But I just can't. That and we have been talking about children of our own. Of course, we can't have unless we do surrogacy or adopt."

"Sounds like you have a lot on your shoulders. Is it worth you going to see Alexandria too?"

Brenton smiled. "I have seen her a couple of times. She is helping a lot. I suggest that once you confirm Roddy, you may encourage him to see her."

I nodded my head. "I think it's a good idea. I could probably do with some head healing too."

Brenton laughed. "As could we all, mate."

Chapter Seven

R^{oddy}

Only two days later, Orion and I found ourselves sitting in a doctor's office waiting to see Dr. Rankin. I was nervous, my stomach was rioting, and I hated the idea that something might be wrong with me. Orion assured me he wouldn't leave, but I wasn't sure he could say that. I was convinced that he would dump me if something was wrong.

I knew it was my stupid hang-ups from being raised as a foster kid that no one wanted. Shit, I grew up in a facility because foster parents didn't even want to be bothered with me. *What did that say?* Add this to it, and I wasn't sure Orion would want me still. Despite what he said. There was so much to consider. Even if I could have kids, there was a chance that I wouldn't be able to keep up with them; my ankles were fused with scar tissue due to the number of surgeries I had, which meant that I couldn't run. *What kind of father couldn't run and keep up with his own children? A shit one.*

Orion reached out and took my hand. "It's going to be alright, Little Wolf," he said, looking into my face.

I breathed in deeply. "I hope so. I just feel sick."

"No matter what happens, I will be right by your side. I'm not going anywhere."

I bit into my bottom lip and nodded my head. "If I can't have children?"

"I'll be staying," Orion answered without missing a beat.

I searched his face, but all I could see was honesty. *Did he mean it? Would he be the one person in my life that wouldn't walk away if it got too hard?* That wasn't fair, Zale, Bronson, and Sarria hadn't walked away from me either, but they were equally as fucked up.

"Roddy and Orion," an elderly doctor called as he entered the waiting area. Orion stood and gave me a small smile. I stood uncertainly and followed quietly behind my mate. This was it. I was going to find out what was wrong with me. Like my body needed anything more wrong with me.

"Hello, now which is which?" the doctor asked as we stepped into his office, and he closed the door behind us.

"I'm Roddy; this is my mate, Orion," I said quietly. Doctors were something I was well versed at talking to. I'd seen so many of them throughout my life. At one stage, I considered becoming a doctor because I seemed to know all the jargon anyway.

"It's lovely to meet the both of you. My name is Dr. Rankin. Why don't you both sit and tell me what you've come in for today?"

I turned and sat in one of the vacant seats while Orion took the other. My cheeks blushed as I was about to talk about the more intimate parts of my life.

"Orion and I have only just become mated. I'd never been with anyone before Orion, and well, I always thought I was an omega, but I grew a knot."

Dr. Rankin nodded as he listened, but the look on his face was utterly professional. It made it a lot easier to share my problem.

"How old were you when you had your first heat?"

"I was seventeen, I think."

"You think? You weren't sure?"

I sighed and shook my head before quickly glancing over at Orion. This was so fucking embarrassing.

"I grew up in foster care. There were only two omegas, me and my best friend, Bronson. I saw him go through heat, but he started them when he was about thirteen. When I was seventeen, I woke up one day sweating and itchy. I did what was needed and that took care of it, but it didn't last as long as Bronson's did. Bronson told me that he thought I was in my first heat. After that, I went on heat suppressants and hadn't had them since."

Dr. Rankin nodded his head. "And when you met Orion, did that push you into a heat?"

I glanced at Orion and frowned back at the doctor before shaking my head. "No. I mean, I had slick, and I could scent that Orion was my mate, and I felt the urge to mate with him. But I didn't have any symptoms of heat. I thought it was because I was on a suppressant."

Dr. Rankin nodded. "That could have been it. But often, when you find your fated mate, the heat suppressants only will work to a certain point. You say you didn't experience any of the heat symptoms?"

"That's right."

"And you can produce slick?"

"Yes."

Dr. Rankin hummed. "Interesting. I can scent you and see that you are definitely an omega, and the fact that you produce slick is a sign that you are an omega, but there is an alpha scent around you. It doesn't belong to Orion, I can smell his scent, and it's definitely not him."

"My friend Bronson said something similar; he said I smelled different and thought it was just because I was mated, but are you saying it could be something else?"

"It could be," Dr. Rankin said before turning to his computer. "I want to run a few tests if that is okay with you. First, I'd like to do a pregnancy test. But I'd also like to do some scans to ensure that your reproductive organs are all as they should be. I will also organize for a CT scan to make sure there isn't something strange going on in your brain where the omega and alpha brain stems are."

"Okay," I answered, feeling a flutter of worry increase in the back of my mind.

"What will it mean if he isn't an omega?" Orion asked.

"Well, for one, I don't believe that you are an alpha. Not a true alpha. You definitely are an omega, but something isn't quite right. It could mean several things. It could mean difficulty in getting pregnant or may be unable to have children. But it could also mean that an omega's hormones might be too low, and therefore you just need a little boost with some medication. I can't give you a definite answer until we see what is happening."

"I understand," Orion said. "But this isn't likely to kill him?"

Dr. Rankin shook his head. "No, no, nothing like that. You will be able to live quite a healthy life."

I breathed out. It wasn't something I had been worried about until Orion mentioned it. But knowing that my life could be relatively healthy was at least a shining light in all of this.

"Right, let's get you to do a quick wee test, and we will check to see if you are pregnant. Then I'll give you the forms to take to pathology to get some blood and book in for the scans," Dr. Rankin said as he handed me a small jar to pee in.

I stood and went to the bathroom. Once I'd done my business and washed my hands, I hurried back to the doctor's office. My heart was pounding in my chest. I didn't want to get my hopes up, but I knew they were already up. I wanted a baby. I knew I did.

"Okay, let's have a little look," Dr. Rankin said as he took my pee jar and dipped the pregnancy test. "This will take a little moment."

It was like waiting for my execution as we all sat in silence, waiting for the test to show whether I was pregnant or not. The doctor finally lifted the test and glanced down. "Okay, so this is showing that you aren't pregnant. So, let's start our investigations and see what is going on."

I felt like he'd punched me in the stomach. I wasn't pregnant. That meant that there was something wrong. Tears prickled at my eyes, and the need to cut was stronger than ever. Orion reached out and clasped my hand. When I looked over at my mate, he watched me with concern.

Chapter Eight

Orion

I knew the moment the pregnancy test returned negative that Roddy was heartbroken. He'd done well at trying not to get his hopes up, but it couldn't be helped. I had my hopes up too. I was nervous about what the tests would reveal. It was confusing, and the doctor couldn't tell us what to expect until the tests returned anyway.

There wasn't anything we could do until then. But I could see that Roddy was already getting wound up about it.

"What can I do to take some pressure off?" I asked as we drove back to Roddy's home.

My mate sighed and shrugged his shoulders. "I don't know. I feel stupid for feeling so disappointed about not being pregnant. I think I already knew that was going to be the case, but it doesn't take away the sting."

I reached out my hand and entwined my fingers with Roddy's. "I understand. I'm disappointed too. I promise I will do everything in my power to ensure we have children."

Roddy sighed. "Thank you," he said, squeezing my hand.

"You never have to thank me. I'm your mate. I want to make your life full of happiness and love."

Roddy gave a small smile and nodded his head. "What about you, though? You deserve happiness and love too."

I grinned. "Of course I do. But I know that just being with you will do that."

Roddy glanced at me with a slight frown on his brow. "Really?"

"Little Wolf, I adore you. In fact, I think I'm very quickly falling in love with you."

Roddy gasped. "Really? But you barely know me."

"Sure I do. Your favorite color is purple, and you love The Doors."

He barked out a laugh and shook his head. "That is what you base love on?"

"Why not? If Mother fate has brought us together, then hell yeah, I'm gonna let my heart rule."

He hummed. "I think you are a sage man Orion."

I grinned and lifted his hand to kiss him. "You're amazing."

Roddy pulled into his long driveway and slowly made his way to the front of the house.

"We need to talk about what we are going to do with housing and stuff," he said as he killed the engine on the car.

I nodded my head and stepped out of the passenger seat. Roddy climbed out of the driver's seat, and we walked together towards the front door.

"What do you want to do?" Roddy asked as he swung the door open, and we walked into the house. He went straight into the living room and flopped down on the oversized leather couch.

I sat beside him before turning and laying my head in his lap. Roddy chuckled but started to run his fingers through my hair.

"I was thinking, if you're not opposed to it, I'd like to move in here. I know you have all of your work here. Plus, it's such a beautiful house; I can't imagine living elsewhere."

"That would be good; it would make it easier for me to do work. But it would mean you are very far from Shifter Ink."

I smiled and shrugged my shoulders, enjoying the way that Roddy's nails scratched over my scalp.

"I will just buy a car."

"You can always take mine until you get one."

I smiled. "How are you feeling about the tests coming up?"

Roddy breathed in and bit into his bottom lip. "I'm scared."

"What scares you the most?"

"What it will reveal. I keep thinking about what that would mean for us if I couldn't have children. Or if it comes back that there is something worse wrong. Like if it is just a problem with my hormones or something, I can live with it, but what if it is something worse."

I nodded my head. "I understand that. But for one, I'm not going anywhere. If the tests come back that you are full alpha, you can't have babies, or you are growing a second head, I'm still going to be by your side. You will have to tell me to fuck off before I leave."

The idea of Roddy telling me to fuck off hurt more than I could imagine. He shook his head and leaned forward, pressing his lips to mine.

"I'm not going to tell you to fuck off," he said.

Chapter Nine

R oddy

Waiting for the appointment day to come up was a killer. I tried to get some work done, I had a book I was supposed to be narrating, but I couldn't focus, and all the words blurred together. Orion had gone to work to do a couple of pieces he had booked. He said he would reschedule them, but I assured him I would be fine on my own.

The truth was that I wasn't doing well at all. The need to cut was constantly present. I'd managed to refrain for months. But this stress was getting too much. I had a blade in my bathroom, and the thought of that bit of steel cutting into my arm was overwhelming.

I walked up and down my hallway, trying to talk myself out of going into the bathroom and cutting. I couldn't explain how cutting made things better. In truth, it wasn't a healthy coping mechanism, and I'd had many doctors and psychologists tell me it was wrong, but it was the only thing that eased my stress.

Maybe if I just looked at the blade. Perhaps that would be enough. No sooner had I that thought than I knew it was a lie. But it was too late; my feet were already walking through my bedroom to the ensuite bathroom.

I bit into my bottom lip as I stared at the basin. "I shouldn't be doing this," I whispered. It was no use; my hands were already reaching for my blade's drawer. The minute I saw the little tin I kept my blade in, I felt my heart beat harder. The thrill of feeling that knick of pain, the way the blood would ooze and drip down over my skin.

I lowered the seat on the toilet and sat down. Opening the tin, I stared at the blade. Orion's face floated through my mind. He'd seen my scars and hadn't asked me anymore about it. I wasn't sure if that meant he understood, didn't care, or didn't know what to say about it. I wondered briefly whether he would be disappointed in me.

I lifted the blade out and twisted it around in my fingers. My heart was beating a hard throb against my ribs. My fingers itched with anticipation. I wondered if this was what it was like for a drug addict about to take that hit.

I brought the blade to my bicep, between two more significant scars. I bit my lip as I pressed the blade into my skin, hissing over my teeth as that first sting of pain hit my arm. Blood instantly started to bloom. I groaned at the feeling before placing the blade on my skin again and slicing. Blood had begun to dribble down my arm and soak into the jeans on which I was resting my elbow.

Over and over, I sliced into my arm until, eventually, I felt myself relax. I closed my eyes and dropped the blade to the bathroom floor.

I wasn't sure how long I sat there, but I heard the front door open and shut. My eyes flung open, and I quickly stood in panic. Shit. Shit. Shit. I picked up the blade from the ground and promptly shoved it into the tin.

"Roddy?" I heard Zale call out.

"Hang on, I'm just in the bathroom," I called as she rounded the corner.

"Oh, Roddy," Zale sighed. She moved into the bathroom and took my hand gently in hers. "They aren't too deep."

It wouldn't be the first time that Zale had stitched me up. In fact, the majority of the scars that I had on my arms, which required stitching, were done by Zale. She reached under the basin and pulled out a towel. Soaking the corner of the towel under some warm water, Zale turned and dabbed it over the wounds.

"What happened that made you need to cut today?" she asked.

"I got a knot."

Zale frowned and looked up at me. "What do you mean?"

"When I mated with Orion. He wanted to bottom while we mated. And I got a knot. And then every time I fucked him, I got a knot."

"And if he fucked you? Did you produce slick?"

I nodded my head. "Yeah. I didn't get a knot when he fucked me."

Zale hummed. "Have you made an appointment to see a doctor?"

I nodded. "Yeah. He wants to do ultrasounds and tests to determine what is happening. But he didn't have any answers yet. Other than I wasn't pregnant."

"Oh, Roddy, I'm sorry," Zale said as she continued to put pressure on my arm to stop the bleeding.

The front door opened and closed. It was only a matter of seconds before Orion entered the bathroom, and his eyes widened.

"What happened?" he gasped.

"I'm sorry," I whispered.

Zale frowned. "Did you not tell him?" she asked me.

"Yeah, he told me. Little Wolf, why did you feel the need to cut?" Orion asked.

I shrugged, wishing the world would open up and swallow me. I was embarrassed.

"Everything just got on top of me," I admitted.

"Little Wolf," Orion said as he reached out and pulled me into his chest. "Baby, that's why I'm here. I want to share your burden."

"I don't want to be a burden to you."

Orion touched two fingers under my chin and lifted my face to look into my eyes. "You are not a burden. You have a burden on your shoulders, and I want to help carry that."

"I'm sorry."

Orion shook his head. "You don't have to apologize to me. Just let me in."

"I'll try."

Orion pressed a kiss to my lips. "I believe you," he said before turning to Zale. "Hi, I'm Orion."

Zale giggled. "I'm Zale; it's nice to meet you."

Chapter Ten

O rion

I could feel Roddy's nerves from the car's passenger seat as we drove towards the appointment. Throughout the week, Roddy had been put through a series of tests, from blood tests to ultrasounds and a CT scan. There wasn't a part of his body that hadn't been looked at. I hoped that it meant we would have answers.

I reached out my hand and linked my fingers with Roddy's. "It's going to be alright. No matter what the tests reveal, we will work through them. I'm not going anywhere and will be by your side," I said.

Roddy hadn't said much after he first told me that he was worried I would leave him, but I could tell it was on his mind. I wanted to show him that I wasn't going anywhere, but I wasn't sure how to make him believe it.

"Thank you," Roddy said, glancing briefly at me as we pulled into a car spot in front of the doctor's office. "I'm scared."

I smiled, lifted my mate's hand to my lips, and kissed his knuckles. "I know you are. If it were me, I'd feel the same way. But I want you to know that I'm not going anywhere."

"That means a lot. And thank you for coming with me today; I know it was a bit of a hassle to shuffle around your clients."

I shook my head. In truth, it hadn't been a hassle at all. I'd spoken at length with Burgess about what was happening, and he'd understood. He helped me with some clients that were new and wanted small pieces. And those that were regulars of mine were happy to wait when I called them and explained that something unexpected had come up.

"You never have to thank me for that. I will always drop everything to come along."

Roddy smiled and breathed in deeply. "Well, I guess this is it. Hopefully, Dr. Rankin has some answers for us."

I squeezed Roddy's hand and swung the passenger door open before sliding out of the car. When I reached the driver's side, Roddy stepped out and locked the door behind him. I took his hand and led him into the reception of the doctor's office.

We didn't have to wait for very long before Dr. Rankin came out and called our names. Roddy stood nervously, his eyes were wide, and he was chewing on his lip.

"Hello boys, come on in," Dr. Rankin said with a wide smile.

Once we were seated, Dr. Rankin opened his computer and started clicking through images from the ultrasound.

"Okay, so we have all your test results back, and this is what we know. It is scarce and rarely seen, but you have an alpha complex. When you develop in the womb, you develop the birth sac and glands that create an omega. Still, you also developed the glands that make you an alpha. Normally when a supernatural child is conceived, they all begin as alphas. Still, as their brains develop in the birth sac, some will develop the genes needed for an omega. But occasionally, this goes wrong, and a child will develop both."

"So, what does this mean for me?" Roddy asked.

"I'm surprised it wasn't picked up earlier due to all your surgeries; I was sure that a doctor should have seen this, but never mind. What the ultrasound was able to show us here," Dr. Rankin said as he pulled up an image on his computer. "Is that you have a birth sac and the reproductive organs that allow you to fall pregnant. However, you have high testosterone levels, the hormone released in alphas. This is why I wanted you to have the CT scan. I wanted to ensure there wasn't a tumor or something causing this."

Dr. Rankin flicked another picture up on the screen, which was obviously Roddy's brain. "This here is your brain, and this," he said, opening a picture beside it. "Is an average omega brain. In the omega brain, you will find this particular stem here, is missing. This is needed for an alpha; it produces the hormones that make a supernatural alpha.

However, if we look at your brain, we can see that you have the standard stem for an omega, here, but also the stem for the alpha."

"In humans, they don't have either of these stems?" I asked.

Dr. Rankin smiled and nodded his head. "That's right. They have only the brain stem here, which supernaturals have, too, that controls all the nervous system. But they are missing the stems that are used for supernaturals."

"So, I have both an alpha and omega brain?" Roddy questioned.

"You do."

"What does it mean for Roddy? Can he have children?" I asked.

Dr. Rankin nodded his head. "Yes. However, your testosterone levels are too high at the moment, which is why I suspect you got the knot and haven't been able to conceive. We can control that by putting you on hormone replacement therapy. That will help promote your estrogen and allow the omega side of your brain to develop stronger and hopefully will mean you will be able to conceive."

Roddy nodded his head. "I'd like that."

"Wonderful. I'll write you a prescription. But I will want to see you more regularly. To begin with, we need to just keep an eye on your levels and such."

Roddy smiled and glanced over at me. The relief on his face was evident. I was glad; it wasn't too out of whack, which meant an easy solution. Roddy and I would be able to be fathers.

Chapter Eleven

R oddy

After getting home from the doctor's and the pharmacy, I read through the paperwork that Dr. Rankin had given us. I sighed in frustration.

"What's up?" Orion asked as he flopped onto the couch beside me. He had been unpacking some of the boxes we had brought back to my place. He had a lot of movie memorabilia and precious things that we had to find room for in my house. Slowly we were moving him in. It was a lot more complicated than we first thought.

"All of the side effects of this medication are aimed at human women; there isn't anything on here about being a supernatural omega taking it," I complained as I waved the sheet with the list of side effects.

Orion took the sheet from my hand and read over the page before snorting. "Please tell me if you have vaginal bleeding or breast swelling."

"I don't think vaginal bleeding is going to be an issue. Mind you if my dick starts bleeding, I'm going to be a little worried." I barked out a laugh before shaking my head.

Orion scrunched up his nose. "Yeah, that would be terrifying."

"I'll try googling it; maybe that will tell me." I opened my phone and typed into the internet search for supernatural hormone replacement therapy. This medication mainly seemed designed for human women going through menopause. There wasn't a whole lot of information out there for supernaturals.

"Maybe supernaturals don't get side effects?" Orion said as he looked over my shoulder.

"Maybe. I guess if I start to feel weird, I'll just ring the doctor."

Orion nodded his head. "I bet it will be fine."

I sighed and nodded. "I hope so. I wonder how long it will take before I can expect to fall pregnant?"

Orion's grin turned wicked as he looked at me. "Well, I reckon we should start practicing straight away. You know, just in case."

I chuckled and licked over my bottom lip. My cock gave a hard throb in my pants. "Yeah?"

"Mmhmm," Orion answered before he turned on the couch and straddled my lap. I stroked my hands up and down his thighs. His bulge told me how much he wanted to practice, and I really liked the sound of it. Orion leaned forward and pressed his lips against mine, sweeping his tongue into my mouth.

I groaned and moved my hands around his ass, pushing on him and encouraging him to grind against me. Orion kissed down over my cheeks and chin before moving to my neck and nipping lightly over my throat.

"That feels so good," I moaned.

"You taste good," Orion responded.

"Does my blood taste good?"

"So, fucking good," Orion whispered; his breath was shaky, and I knew he was desperately holding himself back from biting me. He hadn't drunk from me since our mating bite, but something about it made me want him desperately.

"Bite me," I whispered.

Orion didn't need to be told twice as I felt his fangs penetrate the skin of my neck. I cried out as my cock erupted in my jeans, and cum filled my underwear. My eyes rolled, and my hands tightened on Orion's thighs as pleasure washed over me in waves. When Orion licked over the wound, I looked into his eyes, which were the deepest red I'd ever seen.

"Fuck me," I groaned.

Orion scrambled off my lap and took my hand, dragging me off the couch. I followed behind him as he led me into the bedroom. The sheets were still rumpled from that morning. Feverishly we stripped from our clothes until we were both naked. The scent of slick filled the air. My cock was still hard and weeping.

"Get on your knees," Orion growled.

My eyes widened, and my cock throbbed at the gravelly demand. I fell instantly to my knees. Orion walked towards me and held the shaft of his dick, rubbing the head along my lips, leaving a smear of precum behind. I opened my mouth and let my tongue fall forward as he slid the head of his cock over my tongue, soaking it with saliva.

Chapter Twelve

Orion

Roddy's eyes were wide as he looked up at me with so much lust. Fuck he was beautiful on his knees with his mouth open. His blood had been so sweet that I almost didn't want to stop drinking. It was something I could quickly become addicted to.

I slapped the head of my cock on his chin, slowly thrusting forward across his tongue. Roddy groaned as my dick filled his mouth. He swirled his tongue around the head before swallowing back my shaft. He placed his hands on his thighs and looked up at me before moving his mouth away from my cock.

"I want you to fuck my face," he groaned.

My eyes flared. Fuck, that was hot. "Okay," I said with a smirk. "Tap my leg if you need me to stop."

Roddy nodded his head and opened his mouth again. I slid my dick into the back of his throat, feeling the muscles tense as he gagged. Tears instantly welled in his eyes, and I thrust my hips back and forth, sliding my cock in and out of his mouth. Roddy continued to hold steady. His dick was hard and weeping, but he didn't touch it, instead paying all his attention to having his mouth fucked.

My balls drew tight, but I didn't want to cum. Not yet, anyway. I pulled out of his mouth and skimmed my fingers over his chin, where drool dripped. Lifting my fingers, I sucked them into my mouth, tasting his saliva.

"Fuck," Roddy whispered.

I moved over to the bed and laid on my back. "I want you to ride me," I said.

Roddy stood at once and crawled onto the bed. His thighs were damp with his slick, and his arousal scent was heady. Moving over to my body, he straddled my lap. With one hand, he directed my cock towards his entrance before slowly lowering himself onto me.

I groaned at the feel of his wet warmth and how his muscles tightened around me, milking everything I had.

"Fuck I wish I could knot you," I groaned.

Roddy moaned. "One day, I'd like to fuck you and my dildo simultaneously."

My eyes widened. "Fuck yes," I said, loving the idea of seeing him so full of dick. Roddy started to move up and down, grinding his dick along my stomach. I reached out and moved my hand up and down his shaft.

Roddy's eyes rolled, and he flicked over his nipples with his thumbs. My balls were growing tighter, and I knew that I wasn't going to be able to hold back much longer. I could watch this man fall apart for the rest of my life.

"Fuck, I'm cumming," Roddy moaned as strings of cum shot from his dick, coating my hand and stomach.

Only then did I let my pleasure release. With a moan, I felt my dick kick as my orgasm took over, and I filled Roddy with cum. One day, he would be pregnant. I couldn't wait for it to happen.

Chapter Thirteen

R oddy

It didn't take long to get into the habit of taking the new medication. So far, I haven't noticed any side effects. Well, nothing that seemed out of the ordinary for me. My muscles were aching, but I think that had more to do with the amount of sexercise I've been doing rather than the medication.

"Hey, Roddy," Brian said as he entered the front door.

"Hey, man," I said as I limped back into the living room.

Brian looked at me with a frown. "Your legs giving you trouble?"

I shook my head. "Yeah, a little, but nothing more than the usual. I've been a bit more active lately," I said.

Brian smirked. "I'm sure you have. Congratulations on the new mate."

I chuckled and waved my hand. "Thank you. So, what have you got for me?"

Brian sat on the couch and started pulling papers from his briefcase. He'd been my manager for the last ten years, and I'd be lost without him. The amount of work I'd picked up since joining teams with Brian had been immense. I could thank him for the majority of my income.

"I have three offers for you. Two books and one movie voice-over."

"Oh cool, what is the movie for?"

"An animation remake of Beauty and the beast. They want you to play the beast."

I gasped, and my eyes widened. "That is amazing. I'd love that."

"I thought you might. They want you to read the script and let them know if you are willing to take the role within a week. The other two, one is a vampire thriller, and the other is a cowboy gay romance."

I nodded, taking the contracts from Brian and glancing over them. It didn't bother me what book genre; I liked them all.

"When do the books need to be done by?"

"The vampire thriller is hoping a three-month turn around while the romance is easy, they basically said whenever."

"Awesome. I'm just doing the last on that Sci-fi one; it should be wrapped up by next week, and then I'm free. So, I'll definitely take on the books. The movie I'll go over, when are they thinking of starting filming?"

"Not until next year."

"Oh, that's easy; put me down for that."

"I thought that might be the case." I grinned and nodded my head. "So, tell me all about your mystery man."

I chuckled. "Not really a mystery. But an amazing guy. He is a tattoo artist at Shifter Ink, a vampire."

"Oh, sexy. How did you meet him?"

"Through Bronson, actually. We were going to have a party at his house so he could introduce us to his friends that he'd made at Shifter Ink and his new mate, and Orion walked in, and boom, the rest is history."

"That's fantastic. I'm really happy for you. Are you happy?"

I smiled and nodded my head. "Yeah, I am. I'm the happiest I've been in a very long time." I winced as a sharp pain shot through my back. "I just wish I wasn't hurting as much."

"Have you been to see the doctor? Maybe you are getting some arthritis in your legs?"

I sighed and shrugged my shoulders. "It's possible. I'll see. I have put it down to everything that has been going on."

"Has more happened than just the mating?" Brian asked.

I liked Brian, and we were close, but he wasn't someone I necessarily wanted to share my inner secrets with.

I smiled and shook my head. "No, nothing too bad. I'll see the doctor if it gets worse," I said through a yawn.

Brian frowned and cocked his head to the side. "Are you getting enough sleep? I just noticed, but you have big bags under your eyes and a pale face."

I shrugged my shoulders. "Yeah, I've been sleeping pretty solidly," I replied. "Nothing different to before."

"I think you might need to go back to the doctor."

Just then, another sharp pain zipped through my body, taking the breath out of my lungs. I cried out as the pain migrated from my chest to my head. My eyes blurred, and it was like everything was suddenly too bright.

"Shit, Roddy," I heard Brian call just as unconsciousness took me into the darkness.

Chapter Fourteen

Orion

Iver was laid out on my table while I drew on his back in sharpies. Burgess babysat his nephew and nieces once a month. I loved the way that the Rigby family was so close. All the brothers shared babysitting duties to give the dads a chance to have a kid-free day. It made me wish I had family so that it was something I could do with my siblings.

Whenever Iver came in, the son of Burgess's younger brother Bacchus and his mates, Joachim and Anghus, asked for a tattoo. I'd worried that maybe he was going to get too old for them, but it didn't matter how old he got; he still laid up on one of our tables to get a tattoo done. Of course, the fact that he wasn't quite twelve yet meant that he got sharpie tattoos.

His sister McKenna was laid on Elias's table, getting a whole sleeve of fairies up her arm. While Burgess sat playing with their youngest sibling Canea. "So, what made you decide today that you needed a dragon?" I asked.

Iver sighed. "I was thinking about uncle Jericho and wanted to draw something for him. He seemed sad when I saw him the other day."

"This is a really nice thing for you to do. I could've drawn it on paper so that you could give it to him," I said.

"Na, I prefer it on my back. It gives me a chance to relax," Iver said, sounding more like a man than a little boy. In the scheme of things, he wasn't far off being a man. He was growing up so fast. I remembered when he was just a newborn in Joachim's arms, coming in to visit with Burgess.

It felt like it was only yesterday. I couldn't wait for the day to be able to bring my own child in and show them off. I didn't think Roddy was pregnant yet; he'd only been taking the hormone replacement therapy for a few days. I didn't know how long it would take to help his omega side grow stronger, but I figured it would take more than a few days. But in the meantime, I was having fun practicing. And practice we did.

"How has school been going?" I asked as I sketched onto Iver's back.

"Good. We have been working with Scout a lot, and they have been helping us to develop our powers."

Scout was one of the members of the Onyx Rebels. I didn't know a whole lot about them. But I knew that the Devil's Advocates and the Onyx Rebels worked closely to help rescue omegas being forced into breeding facilities.

"Yeah? Have you learned anything new?" I asked.

"Not me; I don't seem to have any physical powers, like being able to move things or that; mine seems to be more about communication with the creator."

"Would you rather have physical powers?" I asked.

Iver shook his head. "No. I was a bit jealous a while ago when I was the only one who wasn't getting physical powers. I mean, we have Five, who can literally start fires with his mind. And then McKenna has learned she can shift, so she has been learning to fly with Jai and Jasper. But then Scout talked to me and told me that I was important. I was a leader, and my abilities were essential for the upcoming war."

"And that helped you?"

"Yeah, it did. I always knew that I would be relied on for the war, but I always thought that meant I would develop more physical powers, like Five or McKenna. So, when it wasn't happening, I got sad. But then, after some discussions with Scout and the creator, I knew that my role in the war would be to lead the army."

I shook my head. This little boy had so much on his shoulders. "And you are okay with that? I mean, that's a lot of pressure," I said, worrying that maybe his family was putting too much pressure on him.

"Yeah," Iver started before suddenly he went stock still. His eyes widened and seemed to be moving as if following something I couldn't see.

"Iver?" I called, looking down at the boy worriedly.

My alarm must have alerted Burgess, who was coming over to my table. Burgess had just reached us when Iver snapped back to reality.

He looked up at me with wide eyes. "Go home, Orion; it's Roddy."

That was all I needed to hear. I stood from my chair, sending it flying backward, and I raced out of the shop and towards where I'd parked Roddy's car that morning. I plucked my phone from my pocket and dialed Roddy's number.

The ringing went on and on before, finally, it went to voicemail. I pressed the call button again as I raced through the streets towards our home. It kept going to voicemail. Something had to be wrong; I knew Roddy wouldn't ignore my calls.

"Shit, please, Little Wolf, please be alright," I whispered.

Tears were stinging in my eyes. I pressed the call button once more, listening to it ring in my ear.

"Hello, this is Roddy's phone," a man said. The sound of panic in his voice was unmistakable. In the background, I could hear other people talking and calling Roddy's name.

"It's Orion; what's happened."

"Oh, thank God, Orion. Roddy collapsed; he hasn't regained consciousness. I rang paramedics; they are here now and getting ready to take him to the hospital," the man explained.

"Alright, I'll meet you at the hospital," I answered before ending the call.

Turning the car around, I drove to the hospital. I knew I'd beat them there, but at least I'd be there and waiting for when the paramedics brought Roddy in.

Chapter Fifteen

I paced back and forth in front of the ambulance bay as I waited for the paramedics to pull in with Roddy. I didn't know what was happening; besides, he was unconscious. My heart was beating out of my chest, and panic had gripped me.

"Orion," a woman's voice called. I turned to see Zale coming running through the doors and reaching out to hug me. "One of the nurses in emergency called me when she heard Roddy's name. I was down as an emergency contact for him."

"Do you know what is happening? Someone answered his phone and told me he'd fallen unconscious and that they were bringing him to the hospital."

Zale shook her head. "That's about all I know, too," she answered just as an ambulance pulled into the waiting bay.

A paramedic jumped out of the driver's side and came running to the back of the ambulance. He opened it while another paramedic worked on setting up equipment. Roddy was on a bed with his eyes closed. Suddenly doctors and nurses came rushing out of the doors towards the ambulance, and the paramedics pulled the bed out.

Roddy's face was so pale, and he wasn't moving. "This is Roddy, twenty-five years old. Had complained of muscle pain to Brian, his manager, suddenly he cried out in pain before losing consciousness," the paramedic started to explain to the doctors and nurses as they wheeled him into the hospital. "His bp is eighty over forty and dropping. His heart rate is sitting at around forty-five beats per minute."

"Wait, you can't come in here," one of the nurses said to me as she tried to push me out of the room.

"That's my mate," I argued.

"Oh, okay, we will need to get some information. Let's step out here; we need to let the doctors do their work."

I wanted to push the nurse out of the way to get to Roddy, but I knew she was right. There was nothing I could do for him.

"What kind of supernatural is Roddy?" The nurse asked.

"A wolf shifter."

"Does he have any medical issues?"

"He was born with club feet; he's had a bunch of surgeries and has just started taking hormone replacement therapy."

The nurse frowned. "What has he started taking it for?"

"He has alpha complex; the doctor prescribed the hormone replacement therapy to try and help his omega grow."

"Right," the nurse said. "Let me tell the doctors this; I'll be right back."

The nurse dashed into the room, where I could see through the small window that the doctors were hooking Roddy up to machines. I chewed on my lip as I watched.

"He's going to be alright. He has to be," Zale said from beside me. I'd forgotten she was even there.

Movement up the hallway drew my attention as I saw Chase and Bronson coming toward us.

"What's happened?" Bronson asked.

"I don't know for sure; some guy answered his phone; I'm assuming it was his manager and said that he'd collapsed and couldn't be roused. The paramedics just said his blood pressure is shallow, and so is his heart rate," I explained.

Chase rubbed his hand over Bronson's back as tears flooded his eyes. My own eyes were burning. I was terrified. *What if this was it? What if I was going to lose my mate before I even had a chance to really get to have him?*

The nurse stepped out of the room and came toward us. "The doctors are stabilizing him; they want to raise his heart rate and blood pressure. Come with me, and I'll show you where you can all sit and wait."

I followed mutely behind the nurse as she led us all out into the waiting area where hard plastic seats were lined up, and the television played some midday movie. I couldn't sit down; I couldn't stay still. My panic was racing through my body, making it impossible to do anything. I felt like I was going to vomit, pass out, or maybe both.

Chase guided Bronson to one of the seats and sat beside his mate, while Zale stood in the corner staring at the door as if willing to open with some news.

"Is this because of the hormones?" I asked, looking over at Zale.

Zale inhaled deeply before slowly letting it out. "It's possible. I don't know for sure."

"What do you think might have happened to him?" Bronson asked.

Zale winced and bit into her lip. "I don't want to say much in case I'm wrong, but it looks like he might have had a stroke."

My eyes widened, and my heart nearly stopped at the thought. That could kill my mate. I didn't know much about medical things, but I learned that a stroke was terrible and that it could mean that Roddy would never be the same again.

Chapter Sixteen

Roddy

There was darkness all around me that occasionally faded and got lighter. I could hear the sound of people talking and beeping during those times. I didn't know what was happening to me, but I knew something terrible had happened. Knowing I wasn't on my own helped. My wolf was a constant companion by my side, bringing me many comforts.

On one of the occasions that I felt the darkness get lighter and was able to hear things going on, I heard Orion's voice begging me to wake up. I tried to open my eyes, but they were just too heavy. I was so tired, even though I felt like I was asleep.

I wasn't in pain, but I could feel that the left side of my body was heavier. It felt like I had weights on my arms and legs. The sounds around me became crisper, and I could understand the voices that spoke around me. I couldn't even say how long the darkness lasted between the times I could hear things. Only that whenever the darkness faded, it became a little brighter, as if I was drifting closer to the surface of consciousness.

"Roddy, Little Wolf, please, baby, please keep fighting," I heard Orion say. The sound of his voice was so loud in my mind. My wolf nudged me, and when I looked down, he pushed his snout onto the back of my leg as if encouraging me to walk forward.

I took a step, and the world started to grow brighter. When I looked over my shoulder, I noticed the darkness was fading away. My wolf pushed on my leg again, and I took another step. This time the sound of beeping machines was loud, and my body felt warm.

I glanced down at my fingers, curling them; I heard Orion gasp. "Little Wolf. Open your eyes, baby," he pleaded.

I twitched my fingers again. I glanced down at the left side of my body, but my arm hung limply by my side. I couldn't move my fingers, no matter how much I tried.

"Roddy? If you can hear me, please squeeze my hand," a woman's voice called. I didn't recognize her voice. I glanced at my wolf again, who seemed to nod in encouragement.

Curling my fingers on my right hand, I squeezed around the fingers I felt against my palm.

"Excellent. Roddy, can you open your eyes for me?" The same woman called.

I blinked my eyes, but nothing seemed to happen. I lifted my right hand to rub at my eyes and tried to blink them again. This time the world came into blurry focus.

"Little Wolf," Orion cried as I felt him place his head on my shoulder. His scent surrounded me in a comforting hug.

I blinked my eyes again and looked around. I was in a hospital room, surrounded by wires and tubes connected to any number of machines. I was no longer in the darkness, and my wolf had retreated to my mind.

I tried to say Orion's name, but it came out as nothing more than a mumble. Frowning, I tried to speak again, but the words just wouldn't form; it was like my tongue was too big for my mouth. I couldn't get it to move in the right movements to make the words I needed.

"It's okay, Roddy; I'm going to get the doctor so they can explain what has happened," the woman said, who I realized was a nurse.

I tried to repeat Orion's name. He smiled tenderly down at me. "It's going to be alright, Little Wolf. Everything is going to be alright."

But I couldn't see how it would be. I couldn't talk. I couldn't speak; I couldn't move the left side of my body; something was wrong. I turned my head to try and lift my left arm, but it wouldn't move. When I closed my right eye, I realized that I couldn't see out of my left. Reaching up I touched my left eye and felt that the lid was closed. My heart started to pound. *What was going on with me?*

"Hush, baby, it's okay. I promise that this is going to be okay," Orion said. Confusion was sinking into me, and I wanted to scream at someone to tell me what was happening.

Finally, the lady returned with a man in a business shirt and a stethoscope around his neck.

"Hello, Roddy; my name is Christopher Morris; I'm a vascular neurologist who has been working on your case," he said as he stepped in beside my bed.

I nodded and mumbled what I hoped would be the words, what happened.

"Three weeks ago, you suffered a very major stroke. We believe it was caused by a blood clot that started in your legs and worked up to your brain. Thankfully the paramedics were able to get you stable enough that we were able to remove the clot from your brain and save your life. However, there are some complications with every stroke. For some, it is minor, but with you, we see left-side paralysis and difficulty in speech. With therapy and working with doctors, most stroke patients can regain their ability to talk and regain a lot of their mobility. It will take time and patience."

Tears prickled at my eyes. I looked over at Orion. This was too much. My mate, he definitely wouldn't want me now.

"Clot," I tried to force the word out, but it came out more like a grunt. I was frustrated and huffed.

"Wait, I've got an idea," the nurse said before she dashed out of the room only to return a few moments later with a pad and a pen.

I smiled, took the pad and pen from her hand, and wrote the word clot with a question mark beside it before turning it to face the doctor.

Dr. Morris nodded his head. "Yes. We believe that you have possibly had the clot in your leg for a long time. Often patients who have a lot of surgery like you have developed clots. However, and I can't be certain because it's not an exact science, I believe that hormone therapy medication caused an embolism, which happens when the clot moves through the bloodstream. Sometimes, it might settle somewhere else and not necessarily cause a problem. And sometimes, it goes to a vital organ in cases like yours."

"How long, hospital?" I wrote on the paper.

"You are going to need to stay here for a few weeks; we first need to make sure that, of course, you don't have any more clots and that you physically heal from the stroke, and then we will set you up with therapy and everything to help you regain your skills."

"How long take?" I wrote before turning it back to the doctor.

"How long will it take for you to regain those skills?"

I nodded my head.

The doctor hummed. "It can take anywhere from a few months to years. Unfortunately, there is no set time frame, but the therapists will work with you at a pace that is best for you."

I sighed. Years. My job was now down the drain. If I couldn't talk, I couldn't work. My voice. It was the one thing I had going for me. The tears prickled in my eyes and started to fall down my cheeks. Dr. Morris reached out his hand and squeezed one of my legs.

"I'll let you have some time to go over everything in your mind and with your mate. I'll be back to see you later this afternoon and will talk to you more about the different therapists you will be working with."

I nodded my head.

"Little Wolf," Orion said quietly. I turned my head to look over at my mate. "I'm not going anywhere."

I tried to smile. It wasn't happening. I couldn't find it in my heart to smile. The need to cut was so strong that it was almost overwhelming, but I wasn't sure it would make a difference.

Chapter Seventeen

Orion

The days were long and hard. Thankfully Burgess had been wholly understanding and told me to take as much time as I needed. He knew that I needed to be by Roddy's side. I was going to prove to my mate that I would not turn my back on him. Enough people had done that to him throughout his life. I wasn't going to be one of them. Every morning I went into the hospital and sat by his bedside. I could see the dark cloud of depression sucking him down further with every day.

I was worried. I didn't know what to do about it. Every doctor and therapist that came to speak to Roddy ended up talking to me because Roddy seemed to tune them out. I didn't know how to help him. Even when his friends came to visit, he appeared to be uninterested. It worried me. This wasn't the Roddy that I knew and loved. This man was sinking under a wave of depression, and I didn't know how to pull him out.

"How did you know that I was in the hospital?" Roddy wrote on the whiteboard I'd brought him on the second day that he was awake.

"I was drawing on Iver, Burgess's nephew. He was born with extraordinary powers, which means he can communicate with the creator. Anyway, he told me to go home at once and get you. I was trying to ring your phone, but it kept ringing out. Eventually, Brian answered and told me that you'd fallen unconscious, and the paramedics tried to save you. So, I went into the hospital to wait for the ambulance."

Roddy sighed and nodded his head before he wiped the board clean and started to write furiously. This was really the most frustrating way to communicate, but this was it until he could talk again.

"Why do you stay?"

I frowned and shook my head. Taking the whiteboard out of Roddy's hands, I laid it on the bed. I reached out and took his hands in mine. He'd managed to gain the slightest movement in his little finger on his left hand over the last few days, but he still had a long road to travel.

"I love you, Roddy. That's why I stay. I'm not going anywhere. I didn't take that lightly when I asked you to be my mate. When we mated, and I said to you, the only way you will make me leave is if you tell me to fuck off, that is what I meant. I don't care whether I have to wipe your ass for you for the rest of your life or chew your food and feed it like a baby bird; either way, I'm going to be right by your side."

Roddy let out a snort before he reached for his whiteboard again. "Just blend my food, don't chew it."

I barked out a laugh at his message. "Deal. So do you still want me?"

Roddy gave me that uneven smile and nodded his head. He grunted, but I understood what he was saying. He wanted me.

"Then I'm not going anywhere," I replied as I leaned forward and pressed my lips to his. We hadn't done anything sexual, mainly because the man was in hospital, but I didn't want to push anything on him. Roddy moaned as I licked over his bottom lip.

I skimmed my hand down over Roddy's chest to his stomach. Breaking the kiss, I glanced down his body to see that he was very much up for anything. I chuckled before glancing back at my mate, whose eyes were wide, and he was watching me with so much lust that I'd just about do anything.

"Want a hand job?" I asked with a smirk.

Roddy's right eye widened, and his pupils flared. He nodded his head before quickly writing on the board. "You think we can get away with it?"

I giggled like a schoolgirl and nodded my head. "If you're quiet."

Roddy reached up and made a zipping motion of his lips. I felt so naughty, but it was like having my Roddy back for a few moments. I would do anything to have my mate back, even if that meant a risky hand job in the hospital.

Reaching under the blankets, I slipped my hand down over his stomach to his boxer shorts before diving under his underwear and circling my palm around his shaft. Roddy hissed at the first stroke, and I grinned up at him. Roddy watched me intensely as I moved my hand up and down his shaft, circling the head and coating my palm in his precum.

Roddy's eyes rolled, and he moaned quietly, thrusting his hips into my hand. I kept an ear open for anyone coming into the room as I continued to work his shaft up and down. Roddy's moans were growing louder, still quiet enough that they wouldn't rouse anyone, but loud enough that I knew he was close. Roddy opened his eyes and looked up at me. He made a noise that told me he was about to cum. I stroked over his cock as I pressed my lips against his, swallowing the moans that fell from his mouth and tangling our tongues together.

Roddy moaned as cum shot from the head of his dick, coating my hand and his underwear. I broke the kiss and lifted my hand from his dick, licking over my palm and swallowing the salty cum. Roddy groaned.

"Thank you," he said slowly.

My eyes widened, and Roddy gasped. "You spoke."

Roddy nodded and tried to say something else, but disappointingly the words didn't come. I could see the heartache on his face when he realized he couldn't repeat it.

"It's okay, baby; it's a good sign, though. And if I have to keep giving you hand jobs to get you to speak, then that's what I'll do," I said with a grin, making Roddy chuckle.

Chapter Eighteen

R oddy

I was the world's most impatient man, and I knew I was pissing off the many therapists they kept sending me. But I was sick of being like this. I hated not being able to communicate. I hated not being able to walk properly. I was fucking fed up with this god damned wheelchair and the crutches I could only use for small spurts.

It wasn't all bad; I was at least at home now. I wasn't eating God-awful hospital food. But I was still a miserable bastard who just wanted to return to the way I was. Part of me was so fucking angry at Dr. Rankin. I know it wasn't his fault. There was no way he could have known there was a juicy little clot in my leg, ready to kill me the minute I started taking the hormone therapy. I still hadn't been able to completely get my head around how that worked. But it happened.

Obviously, I was no longer on hormone therapy, which meant any thoughts of having children were entirely off the table. Not that I minded, there was no way I was going to be able to bring a child into this life while I couldn't talk more than a few words.

I wanted to celebrate the fact that I now could say Orion and a handful of other words, but it never felt like enough. I was sick of writing on the whiteboard. I wanted to get back to work. I had to give up my role for the Beast; I had to pass off the audiobooks to someone else. I felt like I was letting down so many people.

Of course, the authors I worked with were fantastically supportive, and one even set up a go-fund account to help pay for my medical costs. I had to admit I was really grateful to them. But it still wasn't the same. I was just down. Orion didn't leave my side; I think he was waiting for me to finally just snap and end it all. The temptation was there, believe me.

But the day had finally come when Orion couldn't take any more time off work. Even though he said Burgess would happily let him stay home, he'd already taken four weeks off work. I'd encouraged him to return, and now I was sitting alone in the living room.

I'd flipped through every channel on the television, and nothing was holding my attention. I'd tried to open a book to read, but even that didn't grab me. The temptation to go and cut me was so strong, but I was doing my best to resist. I didn't want to disappoint Orion any more than I already had. Even though he said I wasn't a disappointment, I couldn't see how I wouldn't be.

I was lying back on the couch when I heard the doorbell ring. With my crutch under my right arm, I stood on unsteady legs and slowly moved my way to the front door. I wondered if the person would have gone by the time, I reached the front door. But when I swung it open, I saw Burgess standing on the other side with a man that had a completely disfigured face. It couldn't be any of my friends; they always just let themselves in, and so would Brian.

"Hi Roddy, I hope it's alright that I drop by; I made some extra meals so that you didn't have to suffer through Orion's cooking," he said with a grin.

I huffed out a chuckle and nodded my head as I slowly moved out the way of the door. "C. In," I said as I tried to invite both men in.

"Thank you," Burgess said as he crossed the threshold and walked into the living room. "Where is your kitchen? I'll pop this in the fridge."

I pointed to the door that came from the living room, and Burgess turned with a smile before entering the kitchen. I heard him open the fridge and move some things around to fit whatever he had brought in before he returned to the living room. I'd made my way slowly over to the couch and sat down with a sigh. The one thing I didn't think I would get used to any time soon was how much effort it took to do the simplest of things.

"This is my mate Caspian," Burgess said as he sat beside his mate on the other couch.

"Hi," I said with a smile.

"I know it's hard for you to talk, so don't stress too much, but I just wanted to ask how you're doing. I mean, how you're really doing? Not just the bullshit answer that you might give a doctor," Burgess said, eyeballing me with a dare to lie.

I chuckled and lifted the whiteboard. "This fucking sucks," I wrote before turning it around for Burgess and Caspian to read.

"Yep, I agree. The worst part is not being able to do the things you once did," Caspian said.

I nodded my head. Caspian smiled. "It took me about two or three years. Actually, if I'm honest, it took me until I met Burgess before finally, I started to accept that I had a new normal."

I frowned and started to write on the board. "What happened?"

"I was in an accident. I was a firefighter and got trapped in a burning building. I burned over seventy percent of my body. I spent months and months in hospital recovering just from the burns, then I had to have all the skin grafts and therapy to learn how to do things. And that didn't even cover the way people stared at me."

I nodded my head. Suddenly it made me realize that although my life had been burdensome, and I had to face some significant uphill battles, people struggled just as hard.

"What do you do now?" I wrote.

"I work back at the fire station again. I'm just in the call center now, but I'm currently studying to become a paramedic."

"Aw. Some," I said slowly.

"How is the therapy coming for you?" Burgess asked.

I rolled my one-opened eye and waved my hand before giving a thumbs down.

"It's going to take time; stick with it, man. I know it's shit while you're going through it. Some days I hated my occupational and physiotherapist, but, in the end, they were the ones that got me back on my feet."

I breathed in deeply through my nose and nodded my head. "I. Try."

"That's all you can do."

I nodded my head and smiled. I didn't know how Burgess and Caspian knew that I just needed the company today, but somehow, they knew. I wondered if Burgess's nephew Iver gave them the heads up. I'd got a chance to meet him while I was in the hospital, and for a young boy, he was so wise. He'd told me that I would heal, and I would return to a new normal the day would come. I held onto those words for a long time. I needed it. I wanted it desperately.

Orion

The days turned into weeks which turned into months. I went to as many appointments with Roddy as I could. I was so impressed by his strength and resilience. I couldn't help but think if it were me, I would've given up before I even got started. But Roddy wasn't me. He was so fucking intense. He surprised them by how fast he was healing every therapist appointment he went to.

Even six months on, he still needed to rely on this walking stick, but he was growing stronger by the minute. He had some movement in his left arm, but it still hung limply by his side for the most part. However, his left leg was working much better, and although he still had a predominant limp, he could at least walk.

We walked every night after dinner, just around the property line. It was enough to help strengthen his leg. I was still trying to talk him into letting me build a pool in the backyard. The physiotherapist had suggested swimming to continue supporting his leg without putting pressure on it. I was all for the idea. But Roddy wasn't so convinced.

His face was still drooped on the left side, but it was more his eye; his mouth was almost back to normal. And his speech was coming along a lot better. He still spoke very slowly and had to often think hard about the words he wanted to say before he said them. Still, his vocabulary was growing, and he could keep up a basic conversation.

I was so proud of my mate. I told him every day not just how much I was proud of him but how much I loved him. I couldn't believe how lucky I'd gotten by having Roddy in my life, but he was perfect. He still wasn't convinced, and I often caught him watching me to see if I was honest. But every day, I proved to him. There wasn't anyone else for me. Roddy was my mate and my love.

We'd been able to spend a lot of time in the woods that surrounded our home, with Roddy shifted. I'd assumed that if he shifted, it would heal the issues, but the doctors had explained to me in the hospital that it didn't work like that. However, Roddy didn't have the same problems when he shifted. He was weak and walked with a very big limp, but he could move more freely. His arm that transformed into his front leg wasn't paralyzed while he was shifted.

I didn't know if it helped, but I figured we would do anything to try and help him. I could see the frustration that built up in Roddy. Especially when Brian came to visit him. It just made Roddy realize how much he couldn't do. His voice had been his career, and now he had to wait and take the chance that maybe it might come back. It worried me that it might never be like it once was for him and what would happen if he couldn't do the voice acting.

That was a bridge to cross at another time. For now, I was prepared to walk beside my mate and help him heal as much as possible. We'd seen Dr. Rankin again, who had told us that Roddy wouldn't be able to go back on the hormone therapy medication, which meant that, unfortunately, there was a high likelihood that we would never have children.

Well, I say never, but what I mean is that we might never have our own biological children. We were quite a way off before that discussion, but I knew Roddy desperately wanted a child of his own. It hurt to see how much the news had crushed him. It hurt me too, but my mate's health was more important than the off chance we might have of him falling pregnant.

When Roddy was healed, I was happy to look into adopting a child, and one day I hoped to be able to do that. But until then, I was prepared to wait and pour all my time into my mate.

"Hey, Little Wolf," I said with a smile as Roddy entered the room. The one thing that still lingered was how easily he tired out. He didn't go through a day without needing a nap. I knew it frustrated him, but I tried to point out that it was all part of the healing process. His body was working so much harder to walk and talk now; it was only natural that it would tire out much more quickly.

"Hey, sexy pants," he said with a giggle.

"Ohh, I think I like that," I said, wiggling my eyebrows.

Roddy moved over to the couch and sat down beside me. I glanced down at my mate and leaned forward, pressing my lips to his.

"Can I suck your dick?" I asked suddenly.

Roddy gasped, and his eyes widened. "Like you even have to ask," he replied.

I chuckled and crawled onto the floor. We might not have been able to make babies, but by fuck I was enjoying practicing. I reached out for the hem of Roddy's sweat pants and pulled them down to his thighs before slipping them and his boxers off.

His cock was already hard. I leaned forward and ran my nose along his shaft, inhaling the scent I couldn't get enough of.

"Fuck, you are beautiful," I said.

"Are you talking to me or my dick?" Roddy asked with laughter.

"A little of both?" I mused before opening my lips and swallowing his shaft to the back of my throat.

Roddy let out a long moan, and his head rolled back on the couch. His fingers threaded through my hair as I started to bob up and down on his cock, slathering it with my tongue, tasting every inch of him. I rolled his balls in my hand as I slurped on my mate's dick. Fuck I couldn't get enough of this man.

Roddy's hips thrust as I continued to suck him down. Reaching into my sweat pants, I freed my cock and started to jerk myself in time with my sucking.

"Fuck, yes," Roddy groaned. I jerked myself faster so that I could catch up. His balls were tight, and I knew he wouldn't' be far away.

I felt the shaft of his cock begin to swell just as the tingles of my orgasm started to ebb their way over my body.

"Cum down my throat, Little Wolf," I growled, lifting my mouth long enough to utter the words.

"Cumming," Roddy groaned as I got the first spray of salty cum hit my tongue. I moaned around Roddy's dick as I came into my hand. I closed my eyes and focused on my pleasure as spray after spray hit my throat.

Lifting my head, Roddy held his hand out to me. "Lick your cum," he uttered.

I gave him my hand, which he guided to his lips, slipping his tongue through my fingers and licking off the sticky mess. I groaned at sight. He was so fucking beautiful.

"I love you, Little Wolf," I said.

Roddy gave me a wobbly smile. "I love you too."

The End.

Also by S L Davies

Breeding Facility
Memphis
Bacchus
Coltrane
Pax
Raiden
Nash

Devil's Advocates
Lynx
Israel
Jai
Jasper
Arley
Zion
Oakland

KINK
Gunner
Newlyn

Freya
Tanquil

Obsidian Mechanics
Donte

Onyx Rebels
Onyx Rebels Prologue
Hawke

Rigby Brothers
Asher
Burgess
Macklin
Drake
Obsidian

Schiavu
Schiavu

Shifter Ink
Brenton
Chase
Orion

Standalone
Sisters Revenge
Killer Love
Soldiers At War
Second Chances
Bunny
Caged

Watch for more at https://www.amazon.com/~/e/B0832T8F7Z.

About the Author

S L Davies is an Australian Author living in Country, Victoria. She is inspired by the world around her.

Read more at https://www.amazon.com/~/e/B0832T8F7Z.